A
Donation of
Keene State College
Children's
Literature Festival

MAGGIE
THE FREAK

Text copyright 1992 by The Child's World, Inc.
All rights reserved. No part of this book may be
reproduced or utilized in any form or by any means
without written permission from the Publisher.
Printed in the United States of America.

Designed by Bill Foster of Albarella & Associates, Inc.

Distributed to schools and libraries
in Canada by
SAUNDERS BOOK CO.
Collingwood, Ontario, Canada L9Y 3Z7
(800) 461-9120

Library of Congress Cataloging-in-Publication Data
Bunting, Eve, 1928-
Maggie the freak/Eve Bunting; illustrated by Lucyna
A.M. Green.
p.   cm. — (Young romance)
Summary: Maggie worries that there is no boy in her
high school who won't be put off by her athletic
ability or her interest in cars.
ISBN 0-89565-775-9
[1. Athletes – Fiction. 2. Sex role – Fiction.]
I. Green, Lucyna A.M., ill.   II. Title.   III. Series.
PZ7.B91527Mag   1991
[Fic]—dc20   91-17123
                                                         CIP
                                                          AC

MAGGIE THE FREAK

Eve Bunting

Illustrated by

Lucyna A.M. Green

T H E   C H I L D ' S   W O R L D

"*L*et's face it," Maggie said. "I'm a freak." She scuffed her feet in the park grass and scowled at the plastic-wrapped sandwich in her hand. "I'm everything boys don't like. I'm not little and I'm not cute and I'm not giggly."

Rita stopped wolfing down her taco. "I think you're pretty cute," she said.

"But you're my friend."

Rita wiped her mouth on a paper napkin. "It's just that you're too good at things, Mag. Things that boys don't like girls to be good at. Like cars, and sports and stuff. And you're not… not…" She searched for the right word and produced it with a triumphant grin. "You're not cagey enough about it. You need to hide it a bit, Maggie. It's no different from hiding freckles with Cover Stick. Or hiding skimpy lashes under a load of mascara."

"It is too," Maggie said. "It's way different."

"Well, do you have to win everything?"

"I don't know." Maggie looked with disgust at her limp sandwich. The plastic had turned steamy, like a window that had been breathed on. "I don't try to win. It's just that when I do something I have to put everything into it. That's the fun of it. And then, somehow, I end up winning."

Rita tossed her yellow taco paper in the trash can. "Course, you're pretty big and strong too. That helps."

"Thanks a lot," Maggie said. "That's what I told you already. I'm a freak."

"What I want to know is what you're going to do today about Todd Quinn," Rita asked. "And don't forget what happened before with Frank Jacobs."

Maggie would never forget what happened before with Frank Jacobs. The whole thing seemed incredible now. And the most incredible thing was that she'd been wild about him in the first place. And he'd acted like he'd liked her too. Until the day she'd outrun him in the two-twenty. He'd even faked a pulled muscle to explain to the world why she'd beaten him. And then he broke the date they had for that Saturday night. He said he had the flu. Flew away, more likely, Rita said.

"Well?" Rita asked again. "What about Todd?"

Todd Quinn! He'd come to Christie High about a month ago from across the bridge in Marin County. He had brown hair that was just a shade lighter than Maggie's own. It was thick and straight and one little piece fell down over his forehead. Each time she saw him Maggie's fingers itched with the urge to stroke it back. Todd was tall, taller even than she was, and he had wide shoulders and a wide, white grin. He stalked around the school hallways with a kind of panther walk, muscles rippling under his T-shirt. Once, when Mr. Winston, their physics teacher, had been talking about "leashed and controlled energy" Maggie got such a quick mental picture of Todd Quinn that she'd snorted aloud and Mr. Winston asked her to leave the room. Was there any way to leash and control energy? Not the kind she sensed in Todd Quinn. And the incredible, fantastic thing was that he had noticed her. Twice he'd sat next to her in the cafeteria. And he'd had to pass two empty tables to get to hers. Once he'd opened the door for her on the way into English class. Rita said all that meant was that he hadn't been at Christie High long enough to pick up the normal bad manners from the other creeps. Maggie knew better. He was going to ask her out. She could feel it. When they were together there was a sort of crackling in the air, like a summer storm.

Why in the world had Coach Sommers set this thing up for today anyway? Maybe Jonny was right. Maybe Coach Sommers did push Maggie too hard. Her brother Jonny was right a lot of the time.

"Aren't you ever going to answer me?" Rita asked.

13

"Todd?" Maggie swallowed. Surely Todd wouldn't be childish and stupid, like Frank Jacobs. He couldn't be. But still. "I'm going to make sure he wins," Maggie said.

"All right!" Rita beamed on Maggie like a mother on a favored child. Then she frowned. "But can you do it, Mag? Honest?"

Maggie closed her eyes. "I'll keep saying to myself, 'Don't try. Let him heave that old shot further than you do. What does it matter?'" The words stuck in her throat. And she wouldn't let herself think about Coach Sommers who'd been a girl herself more than a few years back and who was so sure Maggie could out-run, out-putt, out-jump any guy in Christie High. Maybe any guy anywhere.

"I don't trust you," Rita said. "You mean it now. But when you get out on the field with the shot in your hot little hand…" Rita stood up. "I guess I'd better be there to discourage you." She made the letter C out of her thumb and curved forefinger. "I'll do this to remind you. Stay Cagey, Mag!"

Maggie pitched her unwrapped, steamy sandwich into the trash can.

Rita fished it out, peeled away the wrap and tool a bite. "You know something? When you're real bad at things boys will sometimes let you win. I'm rotten at tennis, right? The other day I was playing with Greg Robins and he kept smiling at me and deliberately smashing all his balls in the net. It made him feel great."

Maggie shuddered. "How gross! How insulting! I'd have smashed that ball right into his smiling face."

"I know you would. But just be careful today. It's not as if that many boys are interested in you that you can just throw them away."

"You're some friend!" Maggie muttered. But she knew Rita wasn't being mean. Rita always just told things the way they were. And she was right. That's the way they were.

*A*nd Rita was going to make sure she remembered the "cagey" bit. When Maggie came out on the field that afternoon there she was, standing by the shot-put ring, her thumb and forefinger curved and raised.

Maggie made the C sign back.

She could see Todd standing with a group of guys over on the sidelines.

Amazing how easily she could pick him out in a bunch. She could have found him in the Super Bowl crowd in ten seconds flat. He wore his blue track suit with the white stripes running up the sides, and she saw him flip his head back and laugh at something someone said. That lock of hair, she thought, and her heart flipped too.

Coach Sommers stood by the putting ring. "Hi, Mag," she called. "How are your quadriceps?"

Maggie grinned. "Great." She flexed her arm, feeling the good swell and ripple of the muscles under the skin. Coach was one of the few people who thought it was OK to ask about a girl's muscles. Most people figured females shouldn't have any. And shouldn't sweat. And shouldn't lift weights. They might strain something. What the something was was never too clear. But for sure it was something girls could hurt and boys couldn't.

Coach Sommers was cool. "It does men jocks good to have a girl to beat them every now and then," she'd told Maggie on the fatal day when she'd outrun Frank Jacobs in the two-twenty.

"Yeah, but it's spooking my love life," Maggie said.

"Top athletes don't have time for a love life. And you can be tops. All we need is to build your reputation." There'd been that strange, tight look in the coach's eyes that Maggie noticed from time to time.

"You're going to beat this guy today," Coach Sommers said now. Her voice and her smile said she and Maggie both knew she would.

Todd had been champion at his last high school. As soon as Coach Sommers had heard about that she'd wasted no time setting up today's "unofficial challenge."

"She can't stand it for a boy to be better than a girl at anything," Jonny had said when Maggie told him. "Don't let her use you, Mag. Don't let Coach Sommers hang her hang-ups on you."

Maggie looked at Coach Sommers now and decided that Jonny was being unfair. Sure, Coach Sommers had had it rough when she was in school. She'd told Maggie. Then all the money had gone to the boy athletes. Coach

Sommers thought that with the right training she might have gone all the way to the Olympics. And she wanted Maggie to have the same opportunities as the boys. That was all.

Now Todd was starting across the field. Maybe she couldn't beat him anyway. He'd be using the fourteen-pound handicap shot against her eight-pounder. That was quite a weight difference. And he was good. But she was too. In competition, with her adrenalin up she could toss that iron ball the way most girls would toss a marble. Down, adrenalin, she told it. Down boy.

Todd's adorable white grin was slanted in her direction. "Hi, Hotshot," he said. "Ready to show me up, huh?"

"Going to do my best," Maggie said. She picked up one of the eight-pounders, feeling the response of her arm, the flexing and bracing of her leg muscles as she balanced, every bit of her readying for competition like a racehorse at the starting gate.

"Yeah, Maggie," a close voice yelled. Maggie glanced over and there was Rita, her thumb and forefinger making the big C. C for crafty, cunning, crooked, clever. Or how about C for chicken? Chicken to take a chance on losing Todd before she ever had him.

"I'm not such a Hotshot," Maggie said weakly.

Coach Sommers laid a hand on her shoulder. "Don't ever talk yourself down, Maggie. Sure you're a Hotshot."

She stepped back. "Each of you take two practice throws. Then we'll have the real thing."

"Ladies first," Todd said. He waved Maggie into the ring.

The sun was hot on her head and shoulders. She hefted the shot in her hand, bent her elbow and felt the coldness of the iron brush her right cheek. She hopped back, spun and putted. Her arm had trouble responding to the unfamiliar message that telegraphed from her brain, the message that said, "Hold it! Don't give it that extra thrust! Keep a check on yourself."

Coach Sommers pulled out her measuring tape and walked to where the shot landed. "Thirty-three," she said. "Good thing it's only a warm-up."

Maggie did a couple of side bends and touched her head to her knees. She straightened to watch Todd, his arms flexing straight and rigid, his legs stretched, the weight coming down on his front foot for perfect balance.

"Thirty-nine," Coach Sommers called.

Maggie's second try was thirty-three again.

"Atta girl, Maggie," Rita called and Maggie knew what she meant. She meant, "You're holding back well, Maggie. Keep it up."

Now they were ready to putt in earnest.

Maggie took off her sweat shirt.

The spectators were quiet. C, Maggie she thought. C for concentrate. C for caution.

"Thirty-seven," Coach Sommers called. "Come on, Maggie! You know you can do better than that."

This time Todd tossed a forty-two and got a round of applause. It was a good length since the handicap shot was two pounds heavier than the normal weight the boys used.

Maggie's second and third putts were both inches short of the forty feet.

"Not bad, for a girl," one of the guys standing around said. He held a protective arm curved across his face in mock fear as Maggie stalked past him.

Todd got a forty-three.

Coach Sommers rolled up the tape. "Didn't you eat any lunch, Maggie?" It wasn't often that Maggie had heard that irritable tone in Coach Sommer's voice. She wouldn't let her eyes meet the coach's in case that tight, hard look was back.

"It was hot tuna fish," Maggie said. "I lost my appetite."

"Looks like you lost more than your appetite," the coach said coldly.

Maggie pushed her arms into the sleeves of her sweat shirt and began walking for the gym. A shadow jogged along the grass beside her. It was Todd. He slowed, matched his step to hers.

"I heard you could putt a lot further than that," he said.

"Yeah. Well, you know how it is. Sometimes you have an off day." She

realized she was striding along with her usual gigantic steps and slowed down. Boys didn't like a girl to walk like a Marathon Ms. She saw Rita scurrying away and hid a smile. Tactful Rita, being careful not to spoil anything that might be happening over here now that Maggie had let Todd prove his male superiority. Not that anything was happening, and they were almost at the gym. And then something was. Something wonderful.

"Say!" Todd's face was a little pink under its tan. He flicked back the piece of hair. "I've been meaning to ask you. That movie, you know the one about the guy who skis up Everest?"

"Down," Maggie said. "I think he climbs up and skis down."

"Yeah. Well it's showing in Still Valley. I missed it the last time around and tomorrow's the last day it's playing. Have you seen it?"

"Uh-uh." She shook her head, every single bit of her waiting tensed and trembling for what she hoped was coming next.

"Like to go with me tomorrow night?"

"Sure." Maggie looked up, and there was a single, heart-stopping second when their eyes met and held. His were the color of his sweat shirt, deep, dark blue, and there was the nicest, shyest something in them. Everything around them seemed to have stopped. All the noise from the playing field, the shouts and splashings from the pool on the other side of the fence. And the summer storm was in the air again, the summer lightning crackling around them.

Maggie wet her lips. "I'd…I'd really like that." Even her voice sounded strange.

"Good." Todd's voice was strange too. "I'll call you tomorrow."

"*H*e's going to call me tomorrow," Maggie told Rita as they walked home together. "He's asked me to the movies."

"See?" Rita held up her finger and thumb. "See what being cagey did for you?"

"Maybe it would have happened anyway," Maggie said.

Rita sniffed. "Don't count on it.

There's no way to figure boys."

Maggie walked alone along the sidewalk when Rita turned off on her own street. She should have been happy, and she was. But something was spoiling things. It would have been so much better if she'd beaten Todd and he'd asked her out anyway. It would have proved something. She wasn't sure what, but something. And she wouldn't have felt such a phony.

Her mom wasn't home from work yet. Maggie put the meat loaf she'd left into the oven, peeled the potatoes and set them on the stove.

Through the kitchen window she saw Jonny working on his old El Camino. He had pulled the engine and was disassembling it to replace the rings. She turned the potatoes to low and went into her bedroom.

The mirror showed her reflection. Did she look feminine or didn't she? And what was feminine, this mysterious thing that seemed to be so important to boys? If it meant being a woman, with woman's feelings and longings, then she was OK. Boy, was she OK. The very thought of how she felt when Todd looked at her reassured her about that. But if being feminine meant that you could only be interested in certain things and that you had to be all the time acting dumb and stuff, then she was in trouble. Maybe she was a freak, like she'd told Rita. And nobody would want her unless she changed. But didn't Todd like her? 'Course, he didn't really know her too well yet, and if she had to keep pretending to be what she wasn't...

"Hey, Mag!" Someone was thumping on her window and Maggie stepped quickly away from the mirror.

"Come on out and give me a hand," Jonny yelled. "I'm getting ready to replace the rings."

Maggie hesitated. A feminine girl now wouldn't rush out to help Jonny. A feminine girl wouldn't want to, would think it yukky. But she did want to. There was nothing in the world neater than the inside of an internal - combustion engine with its pistons and valves and the lovely logic of its tubes and hoses.

"Get a move on, Sis," Jonny yelled.

If she were going to be feminine, try to change, she should be practicing now. But Jonny knew the way she was.

"Coming," she called and changed quickly into her coveralls. The time to watch it was tomorrow night.

But the next night, when she looked in the mirror, she wasn't so sure that she'd started off in the right way. She'd wanted to wear something frilly, something that said, "Hey, look at me! I'm a girl and I'm pretty!" But she didn't have anything like that and her mom's things were too small. She'd ended up wearing her only dress, a pale green skimpy one that deepened her tan and which Frank Jacobs had once told her made her eyes look green as seaweed.

It was about the only nice thing Frank had ever said to her, so she figured it had to be a compliment.

"Did I curl my hair too much?" she asked her mom. "Is my dress too short? My darn bones are so…so long! Tell me honestly, Mom, should I change? Do I look too BIG?"

Her dad peered over his paper. "For goodness sake, Maggie. You don't sound a bit like yourself." He put the paper all the way down. "You don't look much like yourself either."

"Oh crumbs!" Maggie said.

Todd called to say he'd pick her up at seven. He had his brother's car.

At five minutes to seven she decided to change. But it was too late. The car was turning into the driveway.

She ran to the door, realizing at the last second that it would probably have been more feminine to let him ring the bell. To have kept him waiting. To not have acted so darned eager.

And there he was on the doorstep, wearing a pale blue shirt and light pants, the last of thé day's sun spilling across his thick, brown hair.

"Hi," he said.

"Hi." She'd never felt so awkward in all her life.

The car sat at the curb, the engine ticking over. It was a '55 Studebaker, the kind with the fins. "Is it…" Maggie began, and stopped. She'd been going to ask if it was a six-cylinder or a V8. Careful, Maggie. "Is it…your brother's?"

she finished lamely.

"Sure is. He's always working on it. I talked him into lending it to me tonight because…" The white grin just about melted the marrow in every single one of her long bones. "Because tonight's special."

"Oh," Maggie said. Did that mean she was special? Or the movie? Or because the movie theatre was so far away? What? What?

He opened the door on her side and helped her in. She could almost hear Rita saying, "Relax, Mag. He just hasn't been around Christie long enough yet to pick up the bad manners from the other creeps."

Her legs seemed to fill all the space under the dashboard. Nothing but big, bare, brown legs. She tugged at the short, green skirt.

Then they were driving through the suburbs and across the bridge.

"I called to find out what time the show starts," Todd said. His shoulder was awfully close to hers. He drove with one hand cupped around the gear shift and it was hard for her to look at anything else but those long, strong fingers with their squared–off nails. Masculine hands. Secretly she examined her own which were almost as big. Oh, to be little and dainty. Once she'd known an itsy-bitsy girl called Dimity. Oh, to be Dimity! But it was Maggie he'd asked out. And something about the night was special. He'd said so.

"So, since the show doesn't start for an hour, how would you like to drive to Lookout Point? With any luck we might catch the sunset. I've been up there once and it's worth seeing."

"Sure," Maggie said.

They drove in silence. Maggie thought about yesterday's shot putt. Would they be here tonight if he hadn't won?

He was pulling the car on to a narrow dirt road. "This is right, isn't it?"

Maggie looked outside. "I wasn't watching." I was thinking, Todd. Thinking about yesterday, and about you, and about me..."I think there should be a sign. But I'm not sure."

Todd changed into lower gear.

Maggie watched the shrubbery

bump and rattle by. Dust and pebbles bounced up to spatter against the sides of the car. "Bad for the paint job," Maggie said and bit her lips. Feminine girls probably didn't worry about paint jobs on cars.

"You know something," Todd said. "I don't remember the point being this far. We must have come five or six miles from the main road. Maybe I took the wrong turn-off."

He slowed the car, peering ahead, and the car slowed, and slowed and stopped.

"What the heck!" Todd exclaimed. He turned off the ignition and switched it back on. The motor whined and whirred but didn't catch.

Todd switched off the ignition.

"Better wait a few minutes," he said. "I don't want to flood the engine."

Maggie nodded. They sat in the dusky silence. Outside, birds rose, fluttering into the last light.

"I guess we've missed the sunset," Todd said. "I hope we don't miss the movie."

*M*aggie searched for words to make him feel better. "I don't care if we see him climb up Everest anyway," she said. "And he'll come down fast. That's probably only the last ten minutes."

Todd grinned. "You're nice, you know it." He tried the ignition again. It groaned like an animal in pain.

"You're nice," he'd said. Nice! That

gorgeous lock of thick, brown hair was right there, within touching distance. Maggie twisted her fingers together in her lap and stared at the hood of the Studebaker. If only she could lift it, peer inside, see what was happening.

"Don't you...know anything about engines?" she asked Todd. "It might be something you could fix real easily."

"I'll look." Todd pulled on his door handle. "But I'm hopeless with cars. My brother's the grease monkey in our family."

Maggie watched him inspect the engine. He poked at something, scratched his head, banged the hood closed.

Oh wow, Maggie thought. I bet I could. I just bet I could. She found herself tracing the letter C with her finger nail on her knee. Cool it, Maggie. It's OK for his brother to be a grease monkey, or for my brother, anybody's brother. But who needs it in a girl?

Todd was back behind the wheel. "There has to be some traffic up here. Someone's sure to come by."

Maggie nodded. There was something about sitting in a car, way, way away from everyone that made a special closeness, a special excitement.

"I never knew your eyes were green," Todd said. "They're green as grass."

"Thanks," Maggie pleated the edge of her dress. Better than seaweed. Of course emeralds would have been better still. Or limpid pools. But grass was terrific.

"If no one comes in five more minutes I'm going to hike back to the road," Todd said. "We don't want to be stuck here forever." He searched in the glove compartment. "And wouldn't you know? No flashlight."

Maggie nibbled at her thumbnail. No flashlight. In a few minutes it would be too dark to see under the hood. If it wasn't too dark already. And they'd have to hike down to the highway, and Todd would miss the movie that he'd already missed last time around, and the whole lovely night would be all messed up. But what would Todd think? Selfish to sit here when she might be able to make everything right again. Like cheating on him again…doubling up on yesterday, and she knew she couldn't do that no matter what it meant.

She opened the car door. "I know a bit about engines," she said.

As she bent over the open hood she heard Todd come beside her.

"See anything?" he asked.

"Yeah. The coil wire's fallen out of the coil. Probably all the bouncing around we did." She pushed it back in. "You want to try it now, Todd?"

The engine started immediately.

Maggie's fingers were smeared with grease. She held them away from her dress, spread wide apart, as she walked to the passenger side.

Todd turned on the headlights and their white beams silvered the dusty road, made a splintered halo of light in the distance.

"Here." Todd took her hands and wiped her fingers with a Kleenex. "How did you do that?" he asked.

Maggie shrugged. "I like to work on cars." The words were out. The true words. She felt his gaze on her face. Maggie the Weirdo, he'd be thinking. Maggie the Freak!

He held on to her hands and there was no way not to look at him. And there was that wide, white grin, and he was shaking his head as if there was something he couldn't believe.

"You are some terrific girl!" he said, and there was so much admiration in his voice that she could hardly stand it.

"I am? But I'm so...so BIG." She

pulled her hands away and clapped them across her mouth. Had she said that?

Todd's laughter filled the car, surrounded them with warmth.

"Big?" Suddenly the laughter stopped and he had her hands in his again, and her heart was thumping like something in a cage struggling to be free.

"But didn't you know?" he asked softly. "Big is beautiful!" He bent forward and his lips brushed her hair. "Maggie," he said. "We're on our way." He put the car in gear, reversed and headed down the dark, narrow road.

Maggie closed her eyes. On our way, to the movies and to much, much more. How could she ever have mixed Todd up with Frank Jacobs? With anyone? Todd wouldn't have cared if she'd outputted him. She knew that as well as she knew her eyes were green, green as grass. Someday she'd tell him about yesterday and how chicken she'd been in case she'd win. They'd laugh about it together.

Her legs still crowded all the space under the dashboard. She squinted along the length of their good, strong bones. "Take all the room you need," she told them silently. "Big is OK. In fact, big is absolutely, undeniably, beautiful!"